The Monster Shop

Julie Beech

HAZAR
P·U·B·L·I·S·H·I·N·G

It was windy and overcast when Christopher made his way home from school. As he walked, he peered into the windows of the houses and shops along the way.

One particular shop, which Christopher hadn't noticed before, had a peculiar light shining from within. He pushed open the heavy front door and tip-toed inside.

There was no one to be seen and not a sound to be heard. Huge furry coats hung along racks. Shelves were stacked with strange, glimmering hats and enormous shoes. Christopher wondered who would be big enough to wear such things.

Suddenly, the front door creaked open.

Christopher slipped under one of the big furry coats
and watched as a huge creature slowly entered the shop.
He held his breath and trembled in his hiding place as
the monster looked around.

The monster took some of the huge clothes from the racks.

Then, to Christopher's great surprise, it unzipped its purple furry coat and removed it. Underneath, the monster was soft and pink all over. Christopher watched in amazement.

The monster tried on many different kinds of clothes. With each new outfit it scowled in the mirror, letting out an ear-shattering 'Grrraaagh!' But its beaming smile was so friendly that, try as it might, it never looked scary at all.

CURLY WIGS

Just then, there was the sound of bellowing voices. Thunderous
footsteps shook the ground. The monster quickly hid under a pile of
coats—right next to Christopher!

The door burst open and into the shop came two terrifying monsters.
Their evil eyes gleamed red and gold like fire.

'Mallow's in here somewhere,' sneered one of them. 'Come on, Boil. Let's sniff him out and have some fun.'

Christopher was terrified and he could feel the friendly monster trembling beside him.

'There he is!' They pounced on Mallow and dragged him from his hiding place.

'Just look at him, Bristle! He's been dressing himself up to look scary,' said the one called Boil.

'You'll never scare anyone!' taunted Bristle.

They teased and poked Mallow and he cowered into the corner of the shop.

Boil and Bristle finally left and their laughter could be heard fading into the distance. Mallow sank down on to a pile of clothes and cried.

Timidly Christopher crept out of his hiding place. 'Hello, I'm Christopher.'

Mallow looked up, startled to find that he wasn't alone.

'Why were those two monsters being so nasty to you?' asked Christopher.

'They tease me because I've never been able to scare anyone, like all monsters should,' snuffled Mallow.

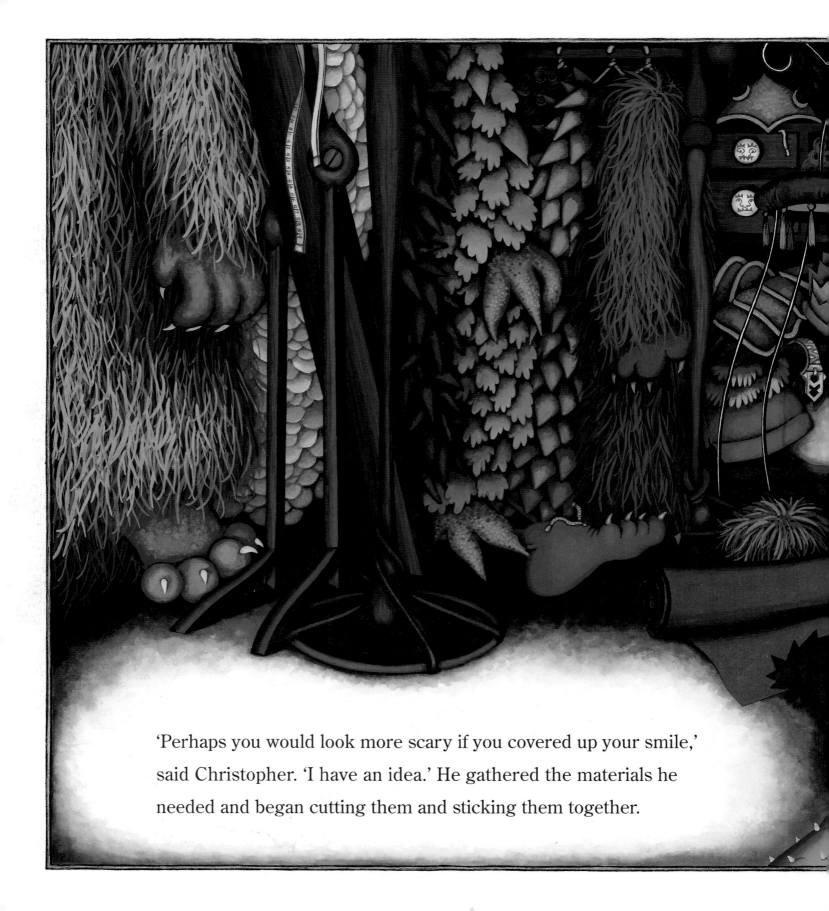

'Perhaps you would look more scary if you covered up your smile,'
said Christopher. 'I have an idea.' He gathered the materials he
needed and began cutting them and sticking them together.

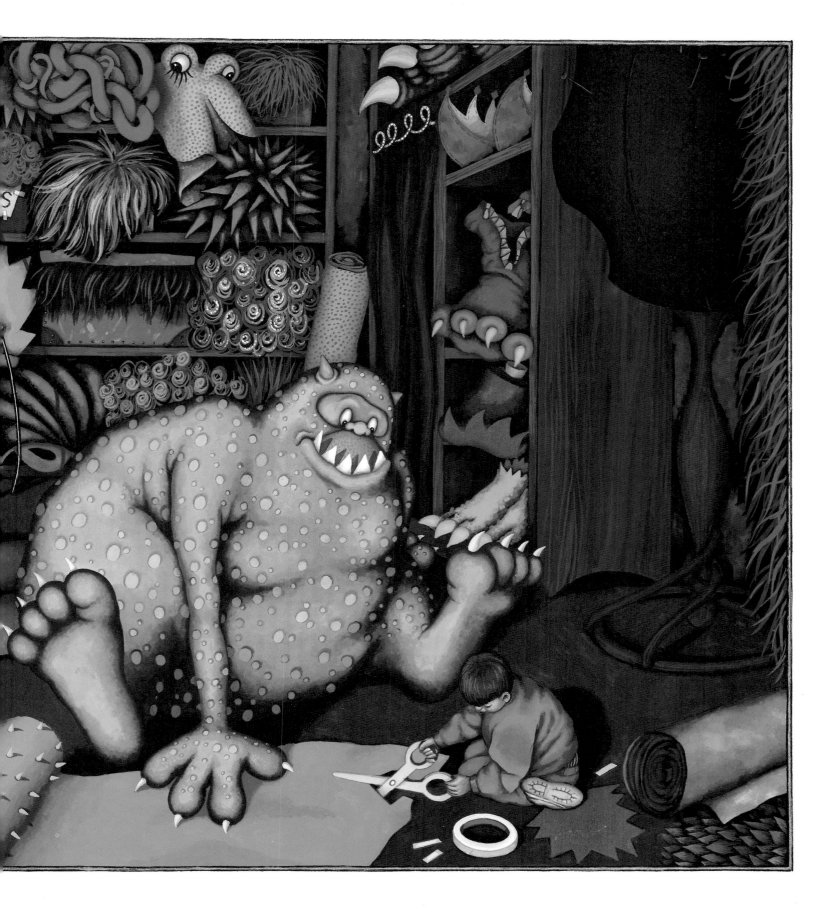

When he was finished Christopher held up a mask for Mallow to see.

'Bend down and close your eyes,' he said. Then he wriggled the mask he had made over Mallow's head.

The monster jumped in fright. He couldn't believe it was his own reflection in the mirror.

'Now you can scare those two!' said Christopher.

'Hurry,' said Mallow. 'If we take the short cut, we can surprise them in the forest.'

'And give them the fright they deserve!' added Christopher.

It was quite dark outside, with just a hint of moonlight. The two friends ran through narrow alleys and winding back streets—places Christopher had never dared venture before.

At last they came to the forest. Mallow climbed into a tree and Christopher hid in the undergrowth. All was quiet.

Soon they heard Bristle and Boil approaching,
still jeering and laughing.

Mallow began to make an eerie noise, quietly at
first, then louder and louder. 'Ooo . . . Eee . . . OOO!'

And Christopher joined in, 'Ooo . . . Eee . . . OOO!'

'Did you hear that?' the two monsters whispered
in unison.

Mallow looked larger than life as he swung down from the tree and howled with all his might.

'OOO . . . EEE . . . OOO!'

And Christopher joined in.

'OOO . . . EEE . . . OOO!'

Trembling with fright, Bristle and Boil panicked and ran away as fast as they could.

Mallow beamed when he removed his mask.

'You were the most terrifying monster ever!' laughed Christopher.

As they hurried back past the monster shop,
Christopher said, 'Let's go home and scare
my mum now. OOO . . . EEE . . . OOO!'
    And Mallow joined in, 'OOO . . . EEE . . . OOO!'

For Stef. J.B. (author)
In memory of Bel. G.J. (publisher)

This edition published in 1997 by Hazar Publishing Ltd,
147 Chiswick High Road, London, W4 2DT.

First published in 1997 by Koala Books,
722 Bourke Street, Redfern, NSW 2016, Australia

Editing, design and production by Margaret Hamilton Books.

A catalogue record for this title is available from the British Library.

ISBN 1 874371 83 0   (Hardback)
ISBN 1 874371 86 5   (Paperback)

Printed and bound in Hong Kong